# Catch It!

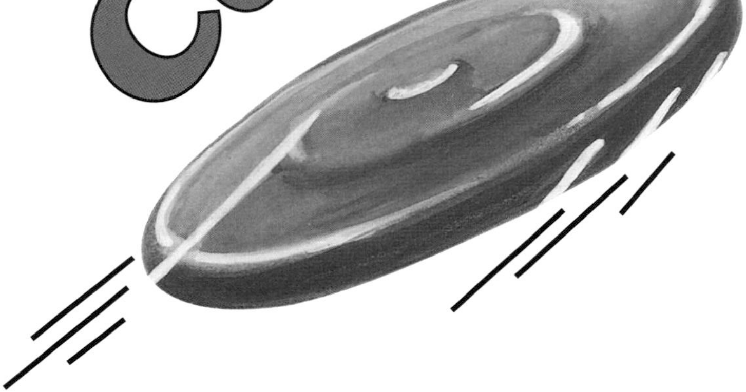

Alison Hawes
Illustrated by Pat Cummings

RIGBY

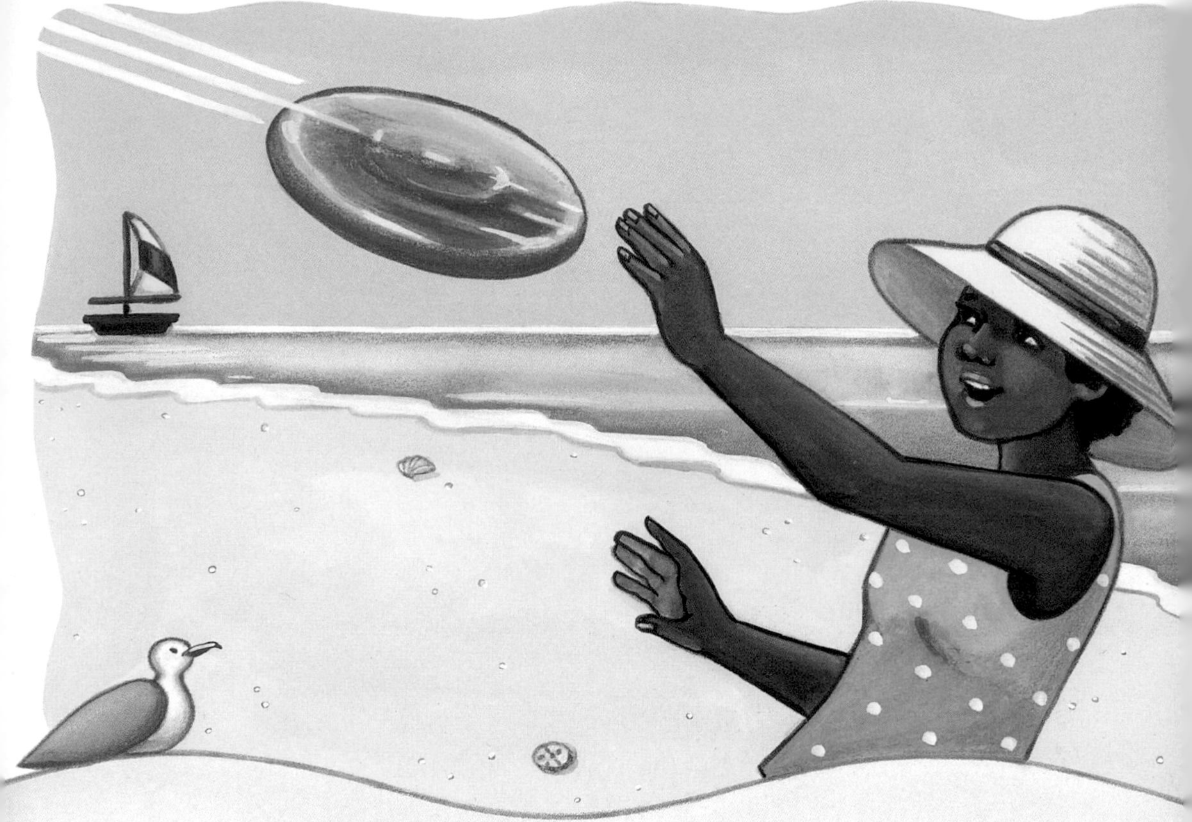

It went to mum.

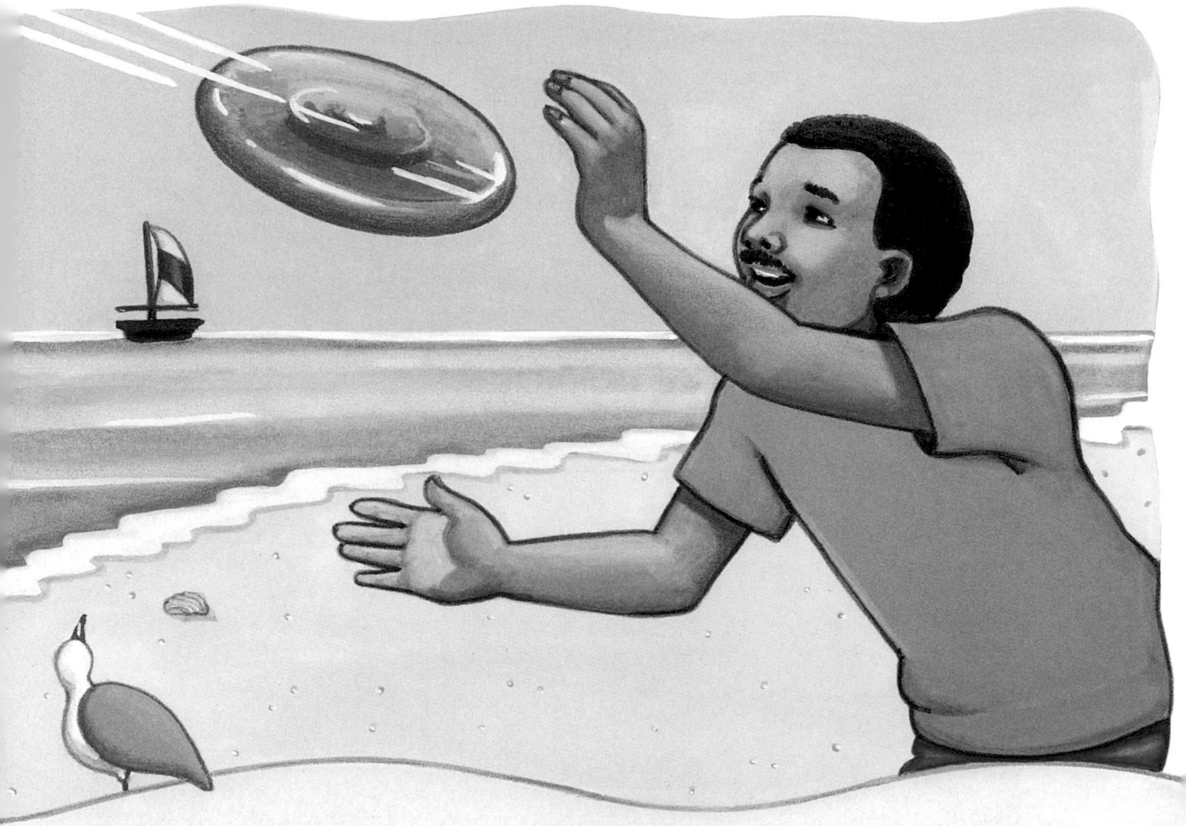

It went to dad.

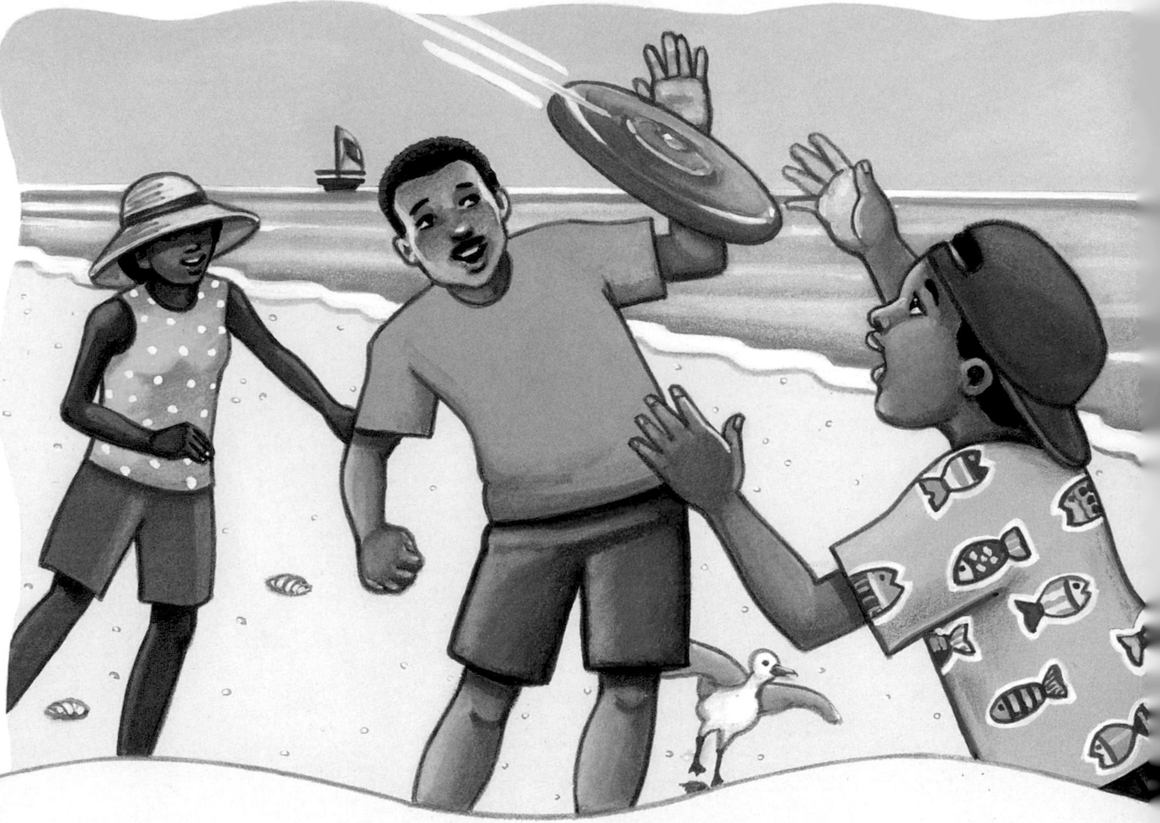

It went to me.

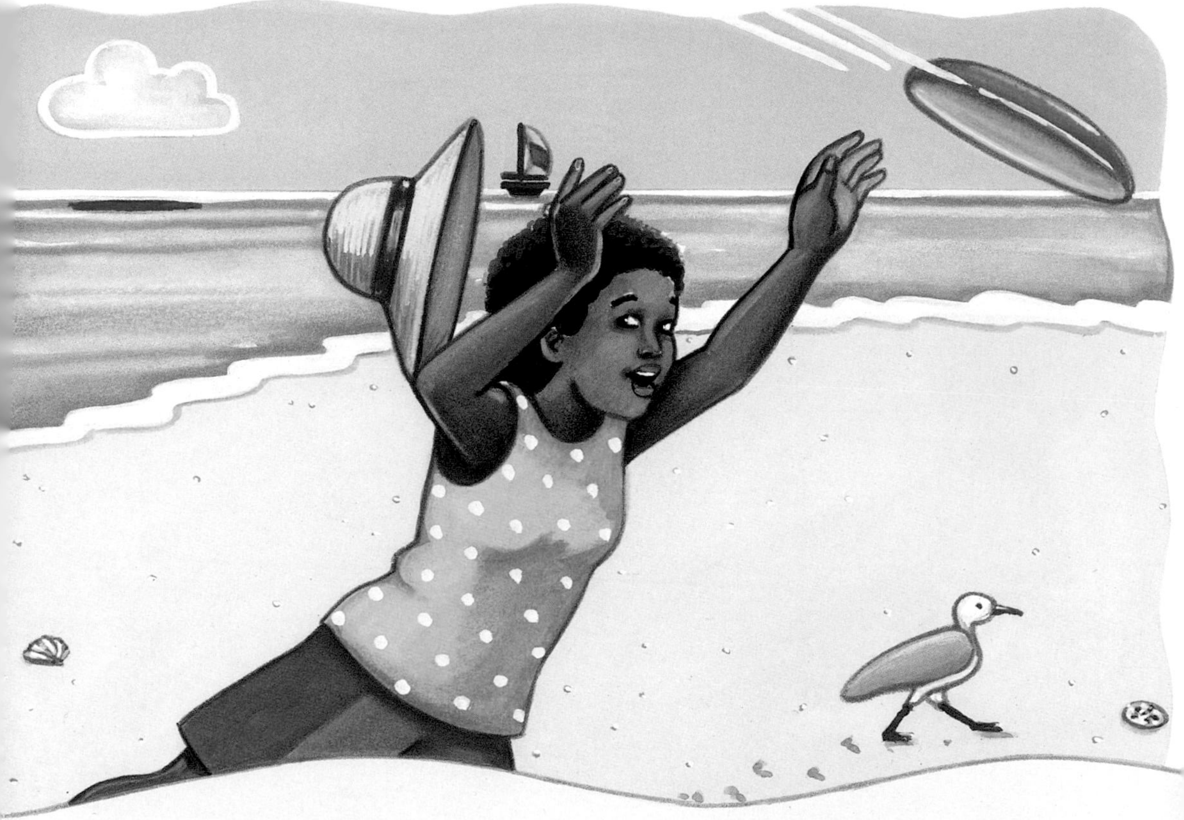

It went to mum.

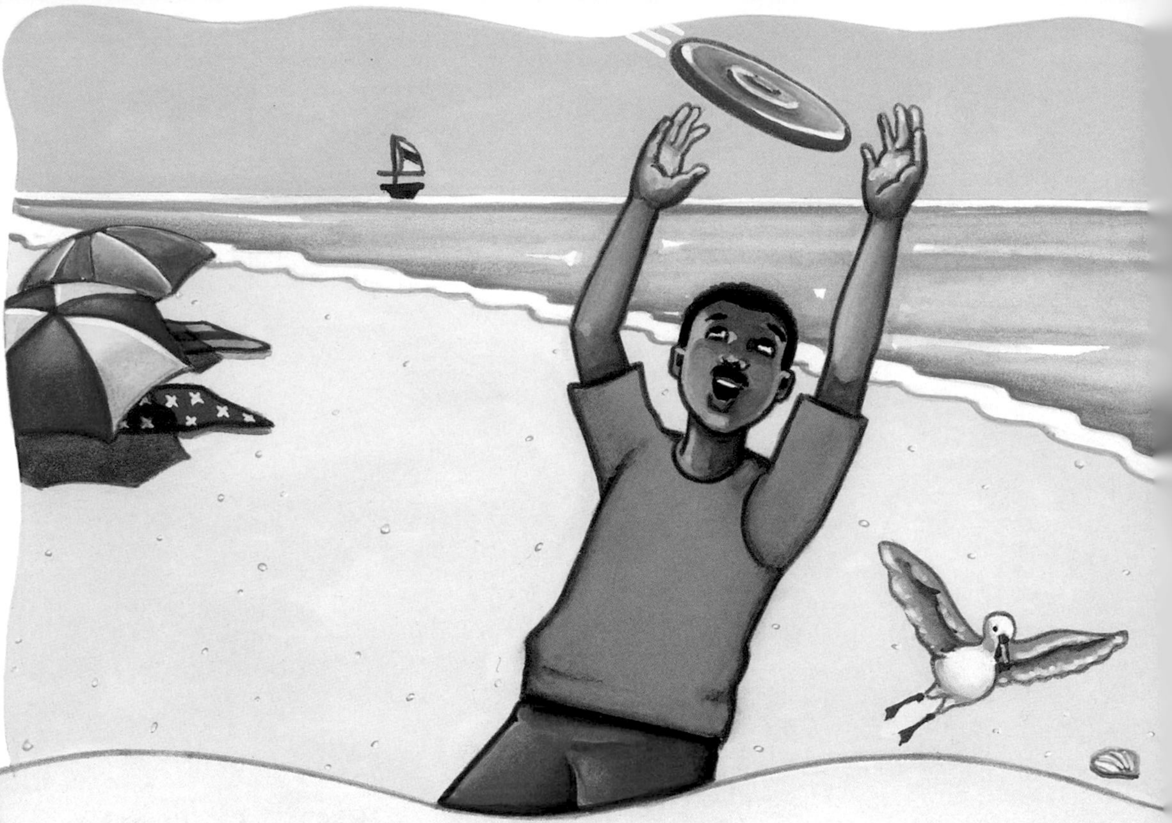

It went to dad.

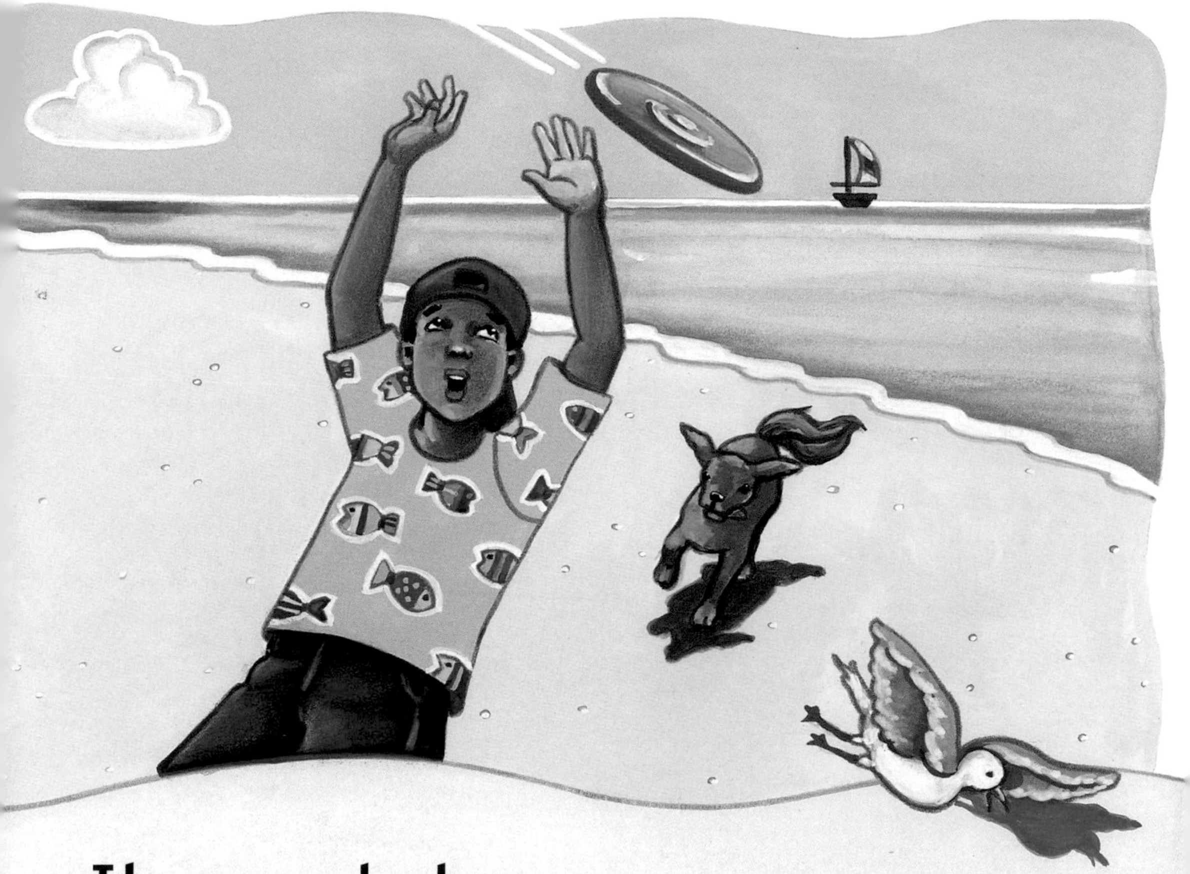

It went to . . .

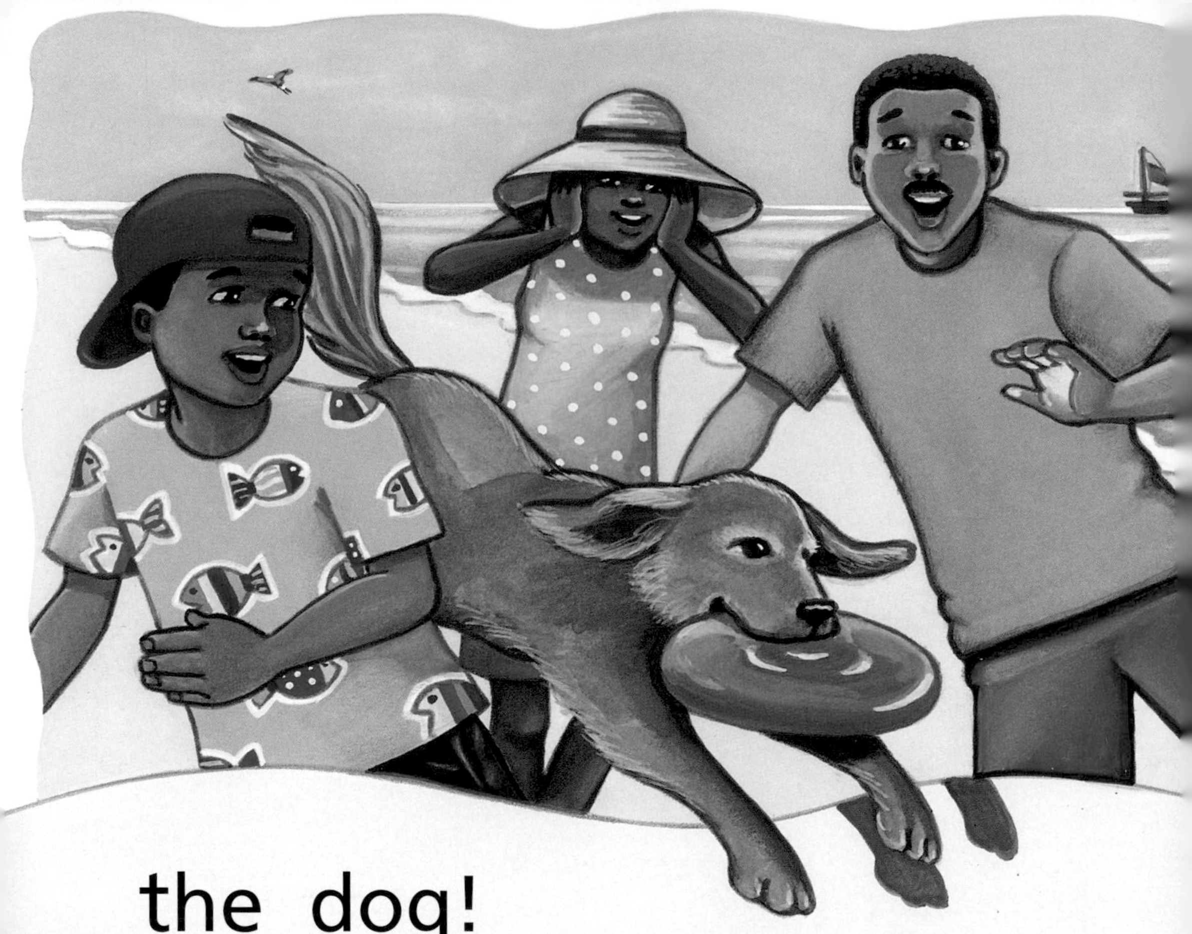

the dog!